One magic
Christmas

A. C. MEYER

One magic Christmas

Translation:
Fernanda Viana

Christmas gift suggestions:
For your enemy, forgiveness.
For an opponent, tolerance.
To a friend, your heart.
For a customer, service.
For everything, charity.
For every child, a good exemple.
For you, respect.
Oren Arnold

For Lu, the sister life gave me.
May your life be magical every day.

Playlist

All I want for Christmas is you — Mariah Carey
Jingle Bell Rock — Glee Cast
Santa Claus is coming to town — Michael Bublé
Rockin' around Christmas tree — Miley Cirus
You make it feel like Christmas — Gwen Stefani
Oh holy night — Christina Aguilera
The first Noel — Glee Cast

One

In a dimension that was far beyond human comprehension, there were beings of light that preserved the order of the universe. They had indestructible powers, mirrored the source of all virtues and passed on all their wisdom to the lower beings, guiding people on their missions. They were in charge of removing the obstacles that opposed the fulfillment of God's orders, driving away the evil spirits that besieged humans to divert them from their end and, thus, keeping the creatures and order of Divine Providence safe. They were very important beings, because they had the ability to pass on knowledge and divine energy. Immersed in the strength of God, these enlightened beings often poured out blessings from above in the form of miracles.

Obviously, Gabriela was not one of those beings. As she listened to Angela, one of the guardians and her advisor, call her name, she wondered: *what have I done wrong this time?*

"Hello?" - She replied, kind of asking, unsure about what the guardian wanted from her. Since she arrived there,

Gabriela has passed through several guardians, but she had not managed to acquire sufficient skill to move to a higher level yet. Every time she had a chance to put all her learning to the test, something happened and things went wrong. It's what happened the last time. She got into a big mess when, due to a *minor issue* with fluency in the language, she ended up causing an accident that made a street to be covered by a ton of chocolate, leaked from a factory in Germany. On Earth, the newspapers reported that it was the fault of a *small technical defect*, but she, Angela and all the other angels and guardians knew *who* the real culprit was. Even today, even though a few weeks have passed, Gabriela was still flushed with embarrassment when she met the Great Guardian.

"Come on, my dear" - Angela's soft voice invited, and she went to her table.

Gabriela approached in awe, as she did every time she entered the room of one of the guardians, but the old woman opened that smile which had the power to calm all angels, from the youngest to the oldest like her. Her vivid blue eyes watched her fondly and she motioned for the girl to come closer.

She smiled, and Angela nodded as she pulled a lock of her short hair, chin length and so white it looked like a cloud, behind the ear. Gabriela thought it was incredible how she looked so youthful, despite the hair that shone like a halo.

"I got a mission for you, young lady" - she said, and her expression was serious for the first time.

"Ah... really?" - Gabriela asked while curling a lock of

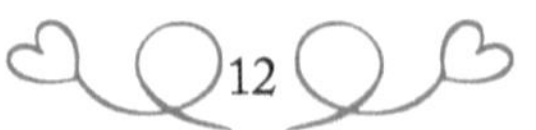

blond hair on her fingertip, already feeling nervous with the weight of responsibility.

"Naturally," she muttered as she rolled her eyes, as if questioning were completely dispensable. Which made sense, since as an apprentice she shouldn't doubt when a guardian said she had a task for her.

I just hope it doesn't involve sweets of any kind, she thought.

"Okay"- she muttered, looking down as she shifted her feet.

"I'm afraid to say, my dear, that this is an incredibly special mission. After the last events, the Great Guardian was determined to demote you to an auxiliary position, but I managed to convince him to give you one more chance. *The last*" - she pointed out.

The young woman shuddered at the words and felt her eyes fill with tears. To have been promoted to apprentice was a great achievement and to return to the auxiliary position would be the greatest dishonor that an angel could receive in the kingdom of heaven. It was like signing a certificate of incapacity and everyone, without exception, would know that she failed her mentors and guardians.

"But... but..." - she started, but the guardian raised her index finger, causing her to shut up immediately.

"You have a sweet and pure heart, Gabriela, and I trust your potential. Besides, one girl must help another, right?" - She blinked and smiled. – "I know you have... certain difficulties, darling, but I need your total dedication to this mission."

Putting her hand on her chest, Gabriela felt her heart

sink. At the same time that it was a great honor to have the guardian's trust, it was a matter of regret to know that this was her last chance to prove that she was worthy of moving forward.

Angela stood up, linked her arm with hers, and led her to the big screen on the other side of the room. Pressing a few buttons, the screen lit up and a beautiful place appeared. Marcela, Gabriela's best friend there - and who had recently been promoted due to a mission successfully executed -, had already told her about this equipment. It was connected to the Earth and transmitted everything that happened there in real time. And it was incredible! That was the first time Gabriela had contact with the equipment and she was delighted.

"What a beautiful place..." - she muttered while watching the illuminated city. Suddenly, she noticed the colonial-style cottages and a shiver of dread reached the base of her column. – "Will I have to deal with the Germans again?" - She asked, alarmed. – "But due to the language..."

Angela raised her hand, interrupting Gabriela.

"This place is called Gramado. It is in the South of Brazil."

"Ohhh" - she muttered, looking back at the screen. – "And what do I need to do this time?"

The guardian looked in her direction, watching her closely.

"Unlike other times, you'll need to go there."

She opened her mouth in a big O. Gabriela never left the kingdom of heaven for a mission. Never ever. All of her missions were executed at a distance and, thinking about it, she suspected that perhaps for this reason they had not worked out very well.

"That's why this is a great mission, darling" - Angela said and focused all her attention on her. – "Your mission is to repair a broken heart."

"A love story?" - The young woman asked. She loved cases involving romance. It was so beautiful to see couples happily ever after!

"Actually, not. It's a... um ... general case."

"Okay..." - she muttered, encouraging herself to continue, even though she had no idea of what a... *general*... case would be about.

"You will be transported there and will need to interact with humans" - she said, and the young woman's eyes widened. – "You will spend time with Samuel and help him to fix his heart."

"But how... how... am I going to do this?"

"You'll know when you get there" - she said, keeping the mystery. But before Gabriela had a chance to protest, Angela continued – "however, my dear, it is very important that you do not forget three things: nobody can know you are from here nor anything related to us; you need to complete your mission by Christmas Eve. When the bell rings midnight, your time on Earth is over."

She nodded, feeling stunned.

"And the third and most important: being in human form, like them, your free will are going to guide your destiny. Stay focused on the mission and be careful with the choices you make."

"Will I have someone's help? And how do I know who this Samuel is? I'm very confused, Angela. And..."

Once again, the guardian interrupted her.

"Everything will be clarified when you are there. And whenever you need me, you will find the answers to your questions in the purity of a child. Now go, my dear. See you at Christmas."

And with the snap of her counselor's fingers, the world she knew disappeared.

Two

First day

Facing the computer, with the text editor open, Samuel closed his eyes as he repeatedly touched the tip of his nose with his index finger, as if inspiration would magically appear. With a heavy sigh, he pushed the swivel chair back and decided to go to the kitchen for some coffee. He had read on some website that the drink helped with concentration and stimulated creativity, but after the fourth - or was it the seventh? - mug of the day, he was feeling more electric than anything else.

He was about to hit the button that would make the coffee maker, his best friend, work when he heard a loud knock in the room.

"Damn it" - he huffed, running a hand over his face, the beard still to be done, and over his hair, which by then was messier than when he got out of bed. He saw no reason to comb or worry about shaving, when he would spend the day alone at home. It is, if he was not disturbed by unexpected and inconvenient visitors.

The knock sounded louder and, distilling a series of curses, he went to the living room and turned the key, knowing who he was going to find on the other side of the thick wood.

"Didn't I tell you to leave me alone, JP?" - He muttered as he saw his editor cross the wooden threshold and enter the cottage as if he owned the place.

Since things started to go wrong, just over six months ago, his life completely turned upside down: his engagement was broken, he got away from his brother - whom he was very close to before *all of that* happened -, couldn't meet the deadline of his manuscript and lost his best friend (who was also his agent) - which justified the presence of his editor there. Since the bombshell had blown off, JP had taken on the responsibility of trying to keep him focused on finishing the manuscript and making worth the big advance he had received.

"As I told you," - JP said, walking into the room and passing him without giving a damn about his hostile words. He was already used to it. Deep down, JP knew that a barking dog doesn't bite. Especially the one over there. – "the cottage, although far from downtown, is very comfortable ..."

Samuca frowned at him, wondering why his editor was acting like a real estate agent, but before he had time to question what was going on, he heard a murmur beside him. He looked away from JP and came across the... *cutest* girl he had ever seen. The blond hair was full and fell in

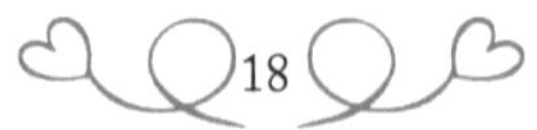

waves over the shoulders. She blinked her eyes, a shade of blue so bright it looked artificially coloured, as she scanned the inside of the cottage. Her features were very delicate, perfectly matching her small stature - at least a foot less than him - which aroused a protective feeling. The same he saw reflected in JP's eyes and which he vowed to himself never to feel since he was made a fool of. Without a doubt, she was beautiful. But more than that, she had a youthful and lively glow that would be able to infect the most serious of mortals.

Except him, of course.

The girl passed him, but ignored his presence, completely focused on the place. She was so dazzled by whatever she was looking at that she seemed to be in front of the eighth wonder of the world and not in a cottage on the ends of Gramado, far from everything and everyone - thank God.

When she stopped a few steps in front of him, he observed her curvy body dressed completely in white, with tight twill pants, T-shirt, jacket and even a Converse-style sneaker, all white. She was almost... shining... if that was possible.

Ah, damn, I'm delusional, Samuca thought to himself. *It must be the fault of that last mug of black coffee I drank*, he said as he slammed the door behind him. Shaking his head, he decided to regain control over his own life. Or at least, his home.

"May I know what the fuck this is?" - He asked with a grunt, and JP stopped talking, looking away from the girl to Samuca. Samuca looked at him angrily, hoping his tone

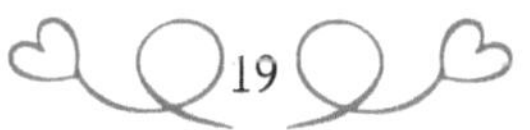

would be ferocious enough to expel them from there. When he looked at the girl, he was surprised to see that she had her hand over her mouth and her eyes wide, as if shocked by his behavior.

JP shook his head in disgust and looked back at the girl.

"Gabriela, this is Samuca." - He waved his indicator in his direction. - "Forgive his manners." - JP said with a gentle smile. – "He has been away from civilization for a long time and must have forgotten how to receive a visitor."

"Visitors are only welcome when invited. That way, I can refuse the presence and avoid this ... *uneasiness*" - Samuca grunted, looking at the girl whose name he knew now.

"I sent you an email two weeks ago, letting you know that I would bring your new assistant. Obviously, you didn't open it, as you do with most of my emails."

"Of course not. I don't have time to waste with small talk, after all, I have a manuscript to deliver" - he replied and looked again at Gabriela, finding difficult to look away.

"Which is not ready..." - JP said, and Samuca shrugged.

"Yet. Besides, I don't need a new assistant."

Managing to stop looking at her, the man passed them both cursing under his breath and was surprised by the crystalline voice that seemed to involve his whole body.

"Of course, you need an assistant," - she said quietly. - "The house is a mess. Your job is late. And you need manners. And a haircut as well."

Her words paralyzed him, surprising him with the boldness of the girl, who barely seemed to have left school,

even though the tone of her words contained nothing but kindness.

"What the fuck are you ..." - he started but lost her attention when the girl looked around the room looking apprehensive. Clearly, she was looking for something. When she seemed to find it, she crossed the room, went to the corner table and picked up a glass ornament.

"That should do it..." - she muttered to herself and took the pot to him. – "Where are those little things?" She asked with a small smile.

"What little things?" - Samuca asked with a frown, and she turned to JP.

"Those little things you used to buy coffee" - she explained to the editor, who was watching her as if she had gone crazy.

After a few moments when the two men faced each other trying to understand what she wanted, JP asked:

"Coins?" - He took out some of his pockets.

"Yes!" - She exclaimed and her whole face lit up with joy. Samuca couldn't help thinking that she was very strange. – "Which is the most valuable?" - She asked JP, who handed her a one Real coin. – "Do you have one of these?" - the girl asked Samuca. He leaned over the coffee table, took two fifty-cent coins and held it out to her, who smiled a satisfied smile. Picking up the coins, she tossed them into the glass jar. – "Very well. It's paid."

Samuca blinked a few times and tilted his head, trying to make sense of what this *crazy woman* was saying.

"What?"

"For each curse, a... coin" - she said and looked at JP, as if to make sure.

JP gave a loud laugh.

"This is going to be really interesting..." - he muttered, still laughing.

Impatient and uneasy with their presence, Samuca let out a long breath and said:

"When you're done with the game, close the door. I have more to do."

As he turned to head towards the kitchen, he was interrupted by the girl's sweet voice.

"JP, thanks for the ride. I promise not to disappoint" - she said with such seriousness that it sounded like she was promising him to establish world peace.

Then it sank in, and he finally realized that she said she was going to stay. There. In *his* house. In his refuge. Where he didn't want anyone to be present.

Ah, not that.

"I don't know what you're up to, but you're not staying here" - he said, knowing he was sounding rude, but he didn't care. All he wanted was solitude back. – "I don't want you in my house."

JP gasped at his rude words, but the girl didn't seem to hear.

"Samuca!" - the editor protested as she started walking around the room, watching everything around her as she muttered something to herself, making considerations about what would be her new home. – "Gabriela will stay with you

until Christmas. It is your deadline for handing over your manuscript.”

The writer mumbled an *I know*, but did not take his eyes off the girl who was walking towards the corridor.

“I don’t need her here” - he protested.

“She will stay to make your life easier. She’ll keep the house in order, type whatever you need, make sure you eat and hand over the freaking manuscript.”

Gabriela turned to the two in indignation, crossed the room again and took the glass jar, holding it out in front of JP. He took a two-Reais bill out of his pocket and threw it in the pot.

She smiled, satisfied, put the pot on the table again and wandered again. Samuca rolled his eyes and protested.

“I don’t want any crazy woman here, JP. I need peace, not a pot freak censoring my words.”

“I’m not a pot freak” - she muttered quietly, without seeming offended by everything the guy said about her. – “Where’s the Christmas tree? She asked, changing the subject so suddenly that it made him confused.”

“What?”

“The Christmas tree. Fifteen days to go before the big night. Where’s yours?” - She asked, looking really curious and even concerned.

“I’ll let you discuss these … um … details” - JP said, taking the boy by surprise with his escape attempt. But before he had a chance to stop him, the editor continued to speak. - “Gabriela, if you need anything, you can call me. Good luck.” He turned and left.

"JP, you forgot your package here." - He went to the door and shouted at the man, who was quickly getting into the car and starting it. *Son of a bitch.*

"I don't see any packages." - Samuca heard Gabriela's voice and turned to find her looking around for something. - "I'm sure he didn't bring any packages..." - She frowned, looking confused. He couldn't help thinking that she looked very cute with that expression.

"You're the package" - he grunted, annoyed to see beauty on that intruder, and slammed the door. As he turned, she was looking in his direction, looking amused.

"I'm not a package, your silly. I'm a woman. Your... um... assistant" - she said, looking proud as she said the words. - "Where's your family?" - She asked.

"In their house" - The answer was just a grunt. She tilted her head gently to the right and watched him, opening her mouth in amazement.

"You don't live with your family?" - He shook his head. - "How do you do to be with your... wife?"

Samuca couldn't help frowning at that word.

"Do I look like the kind of guy who has a wife?" - He asked sarcastically, and she replied, but her words were without irony.

"Not really... you're too moody."

She turned as he huffed and started walking into the house.

"Hey! Where're you going?"

"Getting to work!" - She said excitedly and went down

the hall as if she was about to find a treasure. – "I have a lot to do."

With no alternative, he followed her to prevent that *crazy woman* from doing any damage to his home.

Three

Feeling sick to his stomach, Samuca leaned back in his chair, closed the file he had not typed in and stood up. The sounds of a pan banging coming from the kitchen indicated that Gabriela, also known as the pot freak and his assistant, was preparing lunch. He walked barefoot down the hall, feeling the cold wood of the plank floor against the soles of his feet. He expected to smell homemade food - the only good thing about having a woman living in the house - but all his nose did when he sniffed was the strong smell of burning.

He quickened his pace towards the kitchen and opened his eyes wide when he saw the confusion.

"Holy sh..." - He started cursing and ran away. Gabriela was standing in front of the stove, looking at the flames with a frown and an expression that could be defined as puzzled.

Quickly turning off the fire, he took a dish towel, placed it under the running water, wrung it out, and then threw the damp cloth over the flames, spewing a series of curses.

"What the fuck are you doing with my kitchen? Do you want to set the fucking house on fire?" - He asked shouting, and she walked away, leaving. *Thank goodness she is leaving*, Samuca thought to himself as he put out the fire.

Not so fast, lad.

As he tilted his head trying to figure out what was that misshapen and toasted dough that was out of the pot on the stove - in fact, there was no pan in it - Gabriela went back into the kitchen with the glass jar. Samuca turned to her and blurted out a few more curses, letting her know all the anger he felt.

She was silent for a few moments while moving the fingers of the hand that was free as if she were doing math and when she was satisfied, she said:

"It's thirty-eight."

"What?" - He asked, running a hand through his hair in frustration. – "Thirty-eight what?"

"Little things like that. You have extensive knowledge of bad words. I have never met anyone who knew such a high and varied number."

Samuca looked at her. It wasn't possible. This girl must be playing with him, he thought. But when he looked at her more closely, he realized that her expression was not ironic, mean or mocking. Quite the opposite. Gabriela seemed curious and amused that someone could speak so many bad words. Her face showed total innocence.

Sticking his hand in his jeans pocket, he took out a fifty reais bill that he had forgotten to keep in his wallet and threw it in the damn pot. He must be going as crazy as she

was, he thought as he realized he was obeying her. That crazy woman almost set his cottage on fire, and he was paying for have saying swears. In his own home, for God's sake!

"I don't have change" - she replied when she saw the value of the bill, and he couldn't help but laugh at the ridiculousness of the situation.

"Leave it at the register. I'm sure I'll need it very soon" - he said, shrugging. – "What happened here? He asked, looking again at the stove."

"I followed the instructions on the package ..." - she muttered with a sigh.

"What were they?" - He asked, looking at her.

"Put the pasta on the fire" - she replied, as if it were obvious.

"And the pan?" - He asked, frowning, and feeling a twinge of headache.

"What pan?" - She asked back, confused.

"Jesus," he muttered. - "Have you ever cooked in your life?"

She shook her head, denying.

"But I learn quickly" - she said hopefully.

Feeling defeated, Samuca threw the burnt dish towel into the sink and left the kitchen.

"I can see it..." - he muttered, and she smiled. – "I think we better go out to eat something before you burn my house. Need to change clothes?"

She looked at what she was wearing and followed him as he crossed the hall to the bedroom.

"Change clothes?" - she asked. - "I have nothing to change for."

"Where's your luggage?"

"Luggage?"

"Yeah, you'll be here until Christmas. It's fifteen days... what do you want to wear?"

Gabriela shrugged, confused. She never had to worry about that kind of thing in her home. He watched her, reflecting where that girl came from.

"Did you run away from home?"

"Oh ... no" - she replied, surprised by his question.

"Did you do something wrong? Did you kill someone and run? Are you hiding here?" - He asked, and she opened her eyes wide.

"Of course not. I would be unable to kill someone."

He watched her with half-closed eyes and considered her answer for a while. She was right. She was too clueless to kill even an ant.

"Alright. Stay out here while I change my clothes. And don't get in trouble!" - He said, pointing a finger at her. He slammed the bedroom door as she returned to the living room and sat on the soft sofa to wait for him. He hardly knew that not getting into trouble was what she wanted the most.

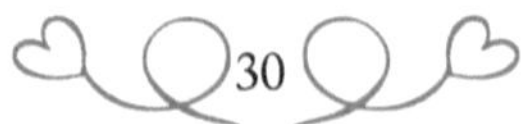

While Samuca drove the car to downtown, Gabriela watched everything with great excitement. It was her first experience in that world, and the girl was impressed with everything she was seeing and feeling. Of course, she had heard about how things worked, customs and traditions, but everything there was much more richer and exciting than in her imagination. The road they followed was full of large trees and it was possible to smell the leaves brought by the gentle wind that hit it. The December sky was very blue and the weather was very different from the weather, always mild, in her world.

She looked away from the guy beside her. He was a very handsome man, but with a very charged aura. It wasn't for nothing that he was heartbroken, as Angela had said. It was impossible that someone as nervous as he could be happy. All those bad feelings, which brought out the worst in him, helped to make his heart bleed with pain, hopelessness and frustration.

After taking the entrance to the city, Samuca took them to a place called Praça do Moinho - a commercial center that brought together shops and gastronomy in one place. After parking the car in a parking space, they got out of the vehicle, and he watched Gabriela look around delighted at the view.

"You never came to Gramado?" - he asked. She reminded him of those tourists who crowded the city and were enchanted by the local beauty. The girl shook her head, looking closely at the Christmas decoration in the stores,

and he couldn't contain his curiosity. - "Where you are from? I couldn't identify your accent..."

"From a place called the City of Angels" - she muttered, concerned not to reveal too much about herself to him. She kept Angela's guidelines in mind, not wanting to disappoint her mentor.

"I've never heard of..." - he said, running a hand over his hair.

"Most people don't even know..." - she completed and diverted his attention. - "And now, where are we going?"

"Have lunch," he replied. - "I will be less irritated to go shopping if my stomach is full".

She smiled and nodded, and he led the way to his brother's restaurant, which he used to go to when he was in town. At this time of year, Gramado was breathing Christmas, with its streets and avenues carefully decorated and lit. The Christmas spirit was present at every corner, and Gabriela was immediately touched by him, singing the songs as they went to the restaurant. It was the time of year that she adored the most, because just like on Earth, in her world they had a big party to celebrate the birth of the Son of God.

As they walked, Samuca looked surprised in her direction. She sang *Silent Night* in a murmur. Since his mother died, Christmas was just another holiday for him and a time to shut up at home alone and drink until he forgot about the hurts, losses and disappointments. That unrestrained joy at Christmas was incomprehensible to him.

When they stop in front of *Nico's Trattoria*, his brother's

excellent and warm Italian restaurant, as she had done throughout the tour, Gabriela showed excitement and delight for the place. Although he was not willing to deal with the family's demands, he knew that he could not go to any restaurant other than this one if he did not want to provoke the third world war.

At thirty-two, Nico was his successful older brother. They've always bein great friends, but ever since Samuca's life imploded, he had been avoiding him. Despite loving his brother, he was not ready to share with him everything that afflicted him... nor did he know if he would ever be. So, it was easier to avoid Nico, his successful venture and his happy love relationship, all that Samuca no longer had.

Not wanting to delve deep into his feelings, he entered the restaurant accompanied by the girl and was immediately received by his brother.

"Long time no see!" - Nico spoke, and Samuca nodded, accepting his brother's greeting. The two shook hands and hugged each other while Gabriela stood beside the two men, delighted by the display of affection between them. After seeing the negative side of Samuca, having the opportunity to witness a softer side - even if it wasn't with her - was inspiring. This was the first time she had seen him smile and she couldn't help thinking that he looked even more handsome when he let his guard down, raised so strongly in front of him. With every moment she spent with him, Gabriela wanted to help him regain faith in himself and in others.

When the two men moved away, Nico looked away from his brother and watched her with a smile.

"And who is this?" - He asked excitedly when he saw his brother accompanied. Since the end of the engagement, Samuca had been closing himself more and more in solitude. That was the first time he had seen Samuca with another woman since everything happened.

"Bro, this is Gabriela, my new assistant" - he said and turned to her. - "This is Nico, my brother". He owns the place.

Gabriela smiled broadly and shook the hand that Nico held out to her.

"It is a pleasure to meet you. I hope my brother is not giving you trouble."

She rolled her eyes with a laugh and was accompanied by Nico, who laughed too, knowing that Samuca was being as difficult as he imagined.

"Come, I'll take you to a table."

After settling them at Samuca's favorite table and indicating the meal of the day as a suggestion for lunch, Nico left them alone and went to the kitchen to take the order.

She watched him as he lost himself looking through the glass of the huge floor-to-ceiling windows and allowed them to see the movement of the street. Despite being a loner, Samuca loved to watch the movement and people. Seeing life pass before him and being part, even for a few moments, of the thread that wove the existence of other beings was an inexhaustible source of inspiration for him,

but it used to drive Letícia, his ex-fiancee, crazy. She complained all the time that he was not paying attention to her, not understanding his need to absorb the world in order to translate it into his words.

Remembering his ex was always accompanied by a feeling of deep sadness and trying to avoid being downhearted, he turned his gaze back to Gabriela. Even though he was uncomfortable with her presence at home, he couldn't help being curious about that girl who looked like some kind of Poliana, always playing the glad game, without ever going out of her mind.

"What brought you here?" - He asked directly, surprising her.

Gabriela blinked, trying to organize her thoughts to explain what he asked without revealing what she couldn't.

"Let's say I have a mission" - she said, looking him in the eye. He realized that this was something she always did: looking anyone in the eye, speaking directly to the person as if she had nothing to hide. - "And I came here to fulfill it..."

"In the meantime, do you work as an assistant to an antisocial writer who doesn't want you at his house?" He asked, scolding himself internally for being rude to her once again.

She nodded and smiled, looking amused.

"Something like that."

"And do you have experience as an assistant?"

Gabriela paused briefly as she considered his question. If she took into account that she were still an apprentice and

helped everyone who needed help in her world, she could say she had experience.

"A little" - she replied, convincing herself that she wasn't lying.

"But you don't know how to cook?" - Samuca raised an eyebrow.

She shook her head, denying.

"It was never... um... necessary."

He was about to ask another question when someone came over and placed the plates in front of them.

"Samuca!" - Josie, the brother's bride, exclaimed. - "How nice to see you here."

She went to him, hugging him tightly. Nico arrived next, with two more dishes.

"I hope you don't mind if we accompany you for lunch."

"Of course, not" - Samuca replied, and the couple settled down.

"What a delicious smell" - Gabriela said, taking a deep breath in front of her plate. Nico laughed, pleased to have pleased the girl.

"It's our mother's recipe for tagliatelle with seafood."

"A family recipe! How beautiful" - she said and clapped her hands.

During lunch, Nico and Josie talked to Samuca and Gabriela, reminding him of several times when he and his brother went out together with their respective brides. The two couples were friends and being there with them made him remember those moments he wanted to forget. The brother changed the subject, touching on a weak point in their relationship at that very moment.

"Did you think about what I asked you for?" - Nico asked in a low voice and a very serious expression.

Samuca looked at his brother and shook his head. That subject was a source of great tension between the two. Since Samuca's engagement ended, the word wedding was removed from his dictionary, which was a big problem for Nico, who insisted, not only that he was present at the ceremony, but that he was one of the best men. Despite knowing how much his brother had been hurt, Nico did not seem to care about Samuca's feelings about marriages and could not accept the fact that he did not want to go to his.

"I won't, man. I told you," - he replied in a grunt. The relaxed posture he exhibited during lunch was now completely closed.

"I can't believe you're going to do this to me," - Nico complained, hurt.

Samuca inhaled and exhaled heavily, annoyed by the conversation.

"I've already explained to you how I feel. I don't want to go. I *can* not go."

Gabriela looked from one to the other, noticing the tension between the brothers. She was sure that this was one of the points of her mission and kept an eye on the events. She looked away from Samuca and stopped at Josie, who intertwined her fingers with the groom's and stroked them, as if trying to calm him down. Gabriela's intuition said that Nico was very hurt by his brother's refusal and the

bride was the one who kept him in balance. It was easy to deduce that Samuca was refusing his brother's request for selfishness or something like that, but while she looked at him, Gabriela could feel all the pain he carried in his chest. He was suffering for a number of things, and his brother's request added even more weight to his pain, which was disguised by bad mood and rudeness.

Nico nodded and excused himself, getting up from the table and removing the plates. When looking away from Samuca, Gabriela was surprised to see that the restaurant - which was empty when they arrived - was now full.

"I think we better get going, Gabriela" - Samuca said, and she nodded with a soft smile. She wanted to comfort him, hug him and say that everything would be okay, but she couldn't. He stood up, followed by her, and placed a kiss on the top of his sister-in-law's head. - "I'm sorry" - he muttered, and Josie nodded and smiled gently at him.

"Everything will be fine, dear... we didn't lose faith" - she said, winked, smiled at Gabriela and left the table. The girl's words struck her deeply. Like Josie, she would not lose faith that she would be able to recover his heart.

For the first time, Gabriela was going shopping and was delighted with the amount of colorful clothes that could be found in stores. In her world, everyone wore white, but there she could wear all the colors of the rainbow if she wanted to. And of course she did.

At first, Samuca was in a bad mood - the result of his usual state of mind along with the annoyance at the disagreement with his brother. He kept his expression upset, something that was now commonplace in his daily life. But Gabriela's joy at each new discovery in her shopping spree influenced him. He couldn't understand how someone could look so cheerful all the time, satisfied with the simplest things in life. And in the third store, he was already smiling and laughing at her amusing comments.

He found it curious how the girl was surprised to see him paying with a credit card, saying that in her city they didn't have that, which made him think that she must have been living in a very rural city, where the facilities of modern life had not arrived. They were leaving the third store when he saw him. He felt the bile rise when their eyes met. They hadn't seen each other in months, since Marco was last at his house to ask for forgiveness, and he put him out. How did you forgive someone whom you trusted your whole life - career, feelings, plans, everything - if that person betrayed you in the most vile way possible? The image of Marco in bed with Letícia still made him wake up at night sweating, feeling as if his body was being torn up and down by a sharp blade. More than the loss of the woman he loved, Samuca felt the loss of his friend. He never imagined that Marco would have the courage to do something like this to him and, despite the fact that the former agent had begged for his forgiveness countless times, he could not forgive or forget.

"Samuca, my friend…" - Marco began, and the look of contempt and disgust that the writer reserved for him made Gabriela shiver from head to toe. There was one more point of her mission, she was sure. Most importantly, it was a vital point in what made Samuca that man hollow inside.

With pure despise in his voice, he looked at the man and grunted.

"Don't you dare call me a friend. You don't know what that means."

"Forgive me please."

He shook his head, feeling his heart bleed again at the memory of the double betrayal.

"Never" - he said and dodged the man who looked devastated. He picked up his pace, which meant that Gabriela had to run after him.

They got into the car and, without delay, he started it and took the road back home in total silence.

Four

Third day

Samuca never felt it was as difficult to write a book as he did with that one. He was a renowned author of fantastic novels, with stories aimed at young audiences whose themes were always intended to encourage his readers, stimulate their skills and address relevant topics to this audience. He had always been a positive guy - he always chose to see the good side of everything... the glass half full, as they used to say -, but after the last events he felt hopeless. It was as if everything he believed in had been destroyed right in front of him. How would he be able to write about characters who fought evil and had total faith that good always won when he himself could no longer believe it?

He ran his hands through his hair in frustration after rereading what he had written in the last five pages. It was rubbish. He was about to erase the five thousand eight hundred and thirty-two words he had written in the past three hours when he heard a soft knock on the door.

Gabriela came in with two mugs of coffee in hand. He couldn't deny it, the girl was funny. Since she was introduced to coffee on her first day there - because, to Samuca's surprise, where she came from she didn't have *this liquid that seemed to have been made by the gods and gives a lot of energy*, in her own words - she had become addicted. From time to time, she made coffee for both of them and took it to the office for him. At first, Samuca was uncomfortable with the invasion, but now... well, now her presence was even welcome to ward off frustration and bad mood.

"Thank you" - he muttered as he took the mug from her and was surprised when took a sip. – "What's in here?" - He asked before taking another sip.

She smiled and, without waiting for an invitation, sat on the gray sofa across the room. Unlike the first day, the girl was not all in white. In fact, she wore a dress so colorful that it seemed to have all the colors of the pantone system. In anybody, that outfit would look ridiculous... but in her, well, it enhanced her beauty even more.

"Judith taught me how to add vanilla essence" - she explained as he frowned. – "Did it get bad?"

"No, quite the contrary, but... who is Judith?"

"Your neighbor."

"My what?"

"Neighbor She lives in the cottage ahead with her husband and young son. They're great people" - she explained.

He watched her with attention. He had been living

in that cottage for months and had no idea that he had neighbors.

She took a sip of coffee and looked towards the computer.

"What are you writing?" - She asked, marveled. She had never seen one of those little boxes he was using and found it incredible that he was able to put in so many words, enough to write an entire book, inside. When Gabriela looked away from the notebook, she noticed that he looked upset.

"I was writing my book, but it's not getting good."

"Why not? What is it about?" - She took the last sip of coffee, put the mug on the table and leaned over, resting her arms on her knees, curious to know what that was about.

"It's about a warrior who crosses a time portal and embarks on an adventure in another world..."

"Oh..." - she muttered, feeling a chill in her belly as she associated the warrior's story with hers. - "And why don't you like it?"

"It's rubbish..." - he said and turned to the computer, selecting all the text he had written so far.

"What are you doing? Why did everything become blue?"

"I will delete"

"Delete?" - she asked.

"Yes, erase everything. Start Over, it's a complete rubbish."

"Oh my God! No way! Wait!" - She asked, not knowing why she had done it. She didn't know anything about warriors' books, but it seemed cruel to him to erase so many writings that could be used for something else if they weren't

for that story... - "Don't you think that anyone, besides you, should read your story? You seem too involved with it to be able to evaluate."

"Are you trying to say that I am unable to evaluate my own work?" - He asked.

"Exactly" - she said and smiled. For the first time, she managed to get a laugh out of him, which made her chest feel warm.

"Very well" - he said when he stopped laughing. Turning to the computer, he generated a file, forwarded it to his Kindle and handed it to her.

"What is it?" - She looked at the equipment in her hand.

"Didn't you say that someone needed to read my text to evaluate?"

She nodded.

"You will read."

"But I don't understand any of that..." - she muttered, looking scared at the equipment, as if it could bite her at any moment.

"You don't need to understand, you need to feel. This is what books do to readers, transport them to other worlds, make them live incredible adventures and feel emotions that would not be possible if it were not through its pages."

"And I'm going to read it here?" - she asked.

"Yes, the manuscript is there now."

He pressed the button that turned on the device and opened the book file.

"Go ahead" - he said, indicating the screen to her and showing her how to turn the pages.

In a very short time, Gabriela embarked on the adventure of the young man who, like her, went on a mission in another world, and got lost in Samuca's words.

It had been just over an hour since Gabriela started reading the manuscript. Samuca had left her alone in the office, huddled on the sofa and, since then, he had wandered around the house like a zombie. He didn't know where he was with his head when he allowed her to read what he had written. Usually, he didn't let anyone read anything he'd written until he was finished and was 100 percent satisfied with the result. But he didn't know what power that girl had that encouraged him to do things he never imagined.

Now he was there, pacing the room, unsure as a teenager in high school, waiting for the teacher to correct his essay instead of the award-winning and renowned writer he was.

Thinking about it made him focus on the big bookcase in his living room. There, in a prominent place, were the books he loved so much and the awards he received over the years for his publications. In a frame, there was a picture of him with two other writers, during a workshop, in which they laughed happily. Where was that carefree boy who enjoyed life and loved to write? When did he lose control of words and give up his passion to become that unhappy and moody person?

The moment you discovered that life is not a fairy tale and

that it doesn't exist a happily ever after, he thought to himself. Marco and Letícia's betrayal marked him deeply. The suffering marks were so deep that he no longer felt capable of loving.

He was about to get up to take the Kindle back - he didn't want to make a fool of himself and let someone read something he knew wasn't right - when he heard the laughter coming from the office. It was a soft, crystalline sound and so beautiful that he felt himself enveloped by the vibration of her laughter.

How long since he heard laughter in that house, he thought. Long long ago...

She laughed again, making his heart soften. Giving up to stop her from continuing to read, he settled himself in the burgundy velvet armchair, rested his feet on the puff of the same color and allowed himself to enjoy that moment. He relaxed to the sound of Gabriela's laughter. Providing joy to those who read his stories was one of Samuca's main goals and it was magical to see it happen so closely.

"And the rest?" - He heard the question behind him and turned around, finding Gabriela with the Kindle in his hand.

"What rest?"

"The rest of the story. I need to know what's going to happen to Robert."

"I'm not finished with it..." - he muttered, and she came around the chair, stopping in front of him.

"What are you waiting for?" - She asked and held out his arms to help him up. - "C'mon, c'mon!"

"Are you thinking this is so? I need inspiration" - Samuca protested.

"What more inspiration do you need besides the incredible story you already have in your hands? It seems like one of the tales that one of our advisors, Miguel, used to tell newbies! It holds so much attention that no one can settle down until it's over."

"What newbies?" - Samuca asked, puzzled.

"From the... um... assistants course" - Gabriela replied, crossing her fingers behind her. Someone had told her that this was a resource to be used in extreme situations and that it seemed to be one of those

"How interesting..." he muttered thoughtfully, but she changed the subject.

"Why did you think it's not good?"

"It's not. I can't find the character's tone. Robert was supposed to be an enthusiastic, courageous, brave and good-hearted hero. Until some part of the book, it is like that, but then..."

"He became boring, moody and disbelieving the world. Do you know anyone like that?" - She asked, and he rolled his eyes.

"Aw shit. I'm not here for you to judge me" - he replied, as she turned, went to the corner table, took the glass jar and held it out to him. - "What?" - He asked. - "Shit is not a bad

word." - She pushed the pot even more firmly towards him. - "Hadn't you left money in favour at the register?"

"It paid your last night's name-callings" - She replied, shrugging. He fidgeted in the armchair, pulled his wallet out of his jeans pocket, took a ten reais bill and tossed it into the glass, which already had a good amount.

"I'll become poor with all of this."

"If you behave, your money will remain in the wallet."

She smiled broadly, and he was unable to remain serious. The two laughed together and she settled on the couch in front of him.

"You know, every storyteller puts a lot of self in his words" - she started to explain. - "While Miguel involved everyone by telling incredible adventures and in such an engaging way, Cielo, another adviser of my..."

"Course?" - he asked.

"That's right. Course Well, Cielo was also an advisor. Despite having a lot of experience, he was not endowed with the grace of patience and his stories reflected that" - she continued explaining. - "The result: his storytelling sessions were not successful among... um... the assistants. And he couldn't understand why. After all, he was as wise as Miguel."

Samuca nodded, waiting to see where she was going.

"Until Miguel explained to Cielo that he was not speaking from the heart. Despite having a lot of knowledge to transmit, he could not only focus on that, he needed to open his heart and allow his essence to be heard. I think

that's what happened. You closed your heart to your words and only allowed yourself to hear that hurt side of you."

She leaned towards him, who was already leaning towards her, with his arms resting on his knees and listening carefully to what she was saying. Gabriela reached out and touched his heart, making him shiver slightly.

"You need to find the Samuca from the beginning of the book. The one who is as bold and brave as the young Robert and who is capable of overcoming any challenge that stands in front of him. He's within you."

Samuca closed his eyes, placing his hand over hers and feeling his voice break as he answered.

"I don't know if I'm capable of that. I lost everything I had and when that happened, my heart bled to death."

With a soft smile, Gabriela muttered:

"Your heart is not dead. I can feel it hitting my hand. In addition, the blood that has been spilled is the perfect color to paint a new love."

She smiled at him, who let a tear slip out of the corner of his eye.

"I don't know if I can ..." - he muttered, and she looked into his eyes, conveying a lot of confidence.

"I know you can. Just try to let love in."

The two were silent for a few moments, until, with a sigh, he stood up and said, before leaving the room:

"I'll try..." - He turned, took a few steps and stopped. - "Gabriela?"

"Yes..." - she said.

"Thank you."

Five

Seventh day

Samuca heard the sound of a radio coming from the kitchen and followed it to there. He found Gabriela beating a cake batter in a mixer that he didn't even know he had. He smiled when he saw kitten-print leggings and a blue T-shirt. She was barefoot, with her hair up and still looked amazing. He was still surprised to see that, in a few days, she - who didn't even know what a pan was - was cooking so well. He would need to enter the gym after the Holidays to regain his shape after so many delicious foods.

"Where did this mixer come from?" - He asked, startling her. She lost her pace and splashed dough in several places. - "It looks old..."

"Oops!" - She recovered the movement of the mixer and looked again at the notebook where the recipe was noted. - "Judith lent it to me."

Gabriela always spoke about Judith, the neighbor he

didn't know, but already knew a lot about. The woman was always guiding Gabriela about the kitchen and by the recipes the girl had been making, she should be a handful cook.

Initially, Samuca thought Gabriela would help him by reviewing texts on the computer, answering emails and things like that, but she was terrible with any kind of more advanced technology. She had no idea what a cell phone was and couldn't understand how a *letter* could travel through cyberspace. But she loved doing culinary experiments, proving to be an excellent cook. And Samuca had to agree that he hadn't eaten so well in a long time.

In addition, at the end of the day, she read the text he had worked on. Afterwards, they discussed the scenes, the characters and she gave him sincere opinions and very relevant suggestions. That was the part of the day he liked best. He hadn't realized that in his eagerness to get away from everyone he felt so alone. And using the events of his book, he could argue with her about feelings that went deep in his soul, using the characters as a defense.

Turning off the mixer, Gabriela took the pan she had already greased with butter and flour and poured the white dough, taking it to the oven. Meanwhile, Samuca got up, collected the dirty dishes, took them to the sink and started washing. They were silent for a while until Gabriela started singing *Jingle Bell Rock*, which she had learned the night before when they watched an old episode of *Glee* on cable. He looked in her direction and smiled. If she wanted to, she could even be a singer. She had a tuned, melodious voice.

"Have you thought about being a singer?" - He asked suddenly.

"Singer? I?" - Her voice was filled with surprise.

"Yes, you sing like an angel" - Samuca said, and Gabriela's eyes widened.

"The what?"

"I said you sing like an angel."

She laughed.

"Have you ever heard angels sing?" - She asked, still laughing.

"Um…no. But if they sang, they would sound like you."

She blushed in a lovely way, and he smiled. He hadn't felt as light in a long time as he did now. They continued to work together while talking. Gabriela asked about his childhood, how he had become a writer and about his relationship with his brother. He told about his mother's death, his passion for books and his brother's restaurant. Talking to Gabriela was good. The girl was a great listener, asking pertinent and non-judgmental questions. It was easy to open up to her, even when she asked about his broken engagement.

"I had a literary event in Curitiba, at *In each page*, a bookstore of Alex, a friend of mine. It was very lively. I hadn't been to a meeting with readers in months, and I used to love these events. I would stay for two more days in the city to have dinner with Alex and Jade, his wife, and also be able to meet some friends - which ended up not happening. I came home the day before."

He paused briefly, but spoke again.

"I decided to surprise Letícia, my fiancee. She had

complained that I was going to travel, as it always did when I had an event related to my work and…”

“Didn’t she like it?” - Gabriela asked, surprised.

“No. She hated reading and thought it was all bullshit.”

“Oh…” - the girl muttered, covering her mouth with her hand, but Samuca continued.

“When I got home, the surprised one was me.” - Gabriela raised her eyebrow. - “She was in bed with my best friend.”

“My God,” - she whispered, and he nodded.

“It was a blow. I truly did not expect it.”

He bowed his head, feeling embarrassed that he had told her that story. What was he thinking when he decided to talk about it?

Gabriela was silent for a few moments and then asked:

“Is that why you became like this?”

“What do you mean?” - He asked, still looking at the floor.

“Bitter, disappointed with life, moody… heartbroken.”

He looked up and all he saw and felt in her eyes and in her voice was goodness and kindness. There was no irony, judgment, or criticism in her voice tone, which encouraged him to continue to open his heart up.

“My world collapsed. Everything I believed in was a big lie. I was betrayed by the woman I thought I would spend the rest of my life with and the friend I had for a brother.”

“I see…” - She leaned back on the kitchen counter and asked, looking much older and wiser than her… *um, how old was she really?* - “You know it’s not your fault, right?”

“What?”

"You are not to blame for what happened."

He closed his eyes.

"If I had tried harder... been a better companion..."

"They would have done the same, Samuca. True love does not hurt or betray. There are things that happen in life to teach lessons and make human beings grow. To mature. But you need to move on. You cannot be forever attached to a hurt. Your world has collapsed, but you are still standing."

"I can't get over it. I can not forget. I can't forgive."

She came over, put a hand on his and muttered.

"Nobody is asking you to do this." - He sighed. - "But you need to forgive. Yourself, and whoever asks for your forgiveness."

Immediately, his thoughts returned to the moments when he met Marco on the street and his ex-friend begged him for forgiveness.

"I can't. I can't go over everything that happened. I can't let them move on as if nothing has happened" - he raised his voice, but she didn't lose her temper.

"You can and should forgive. Not because they deserve forgiveness, but because you deserve peace."

Gabriela's words hit him. They were silent for a few moments until the oven timer went off. The girl released his hand and went to take the cake out of the oven.

"Looks like our snack just got ready!" - she exclaimed, returning to be the cheerful young woman from before, looking nothing like the intense woman who looked at him gently when he opened his heart.

That night, after dinner, Gabriela said she was going out.

"I'm going to Judith's home to return the mixer" - she explained.

"But it's late... can't you return it tomorrow?" - Samuca asked, worried. Although Gramado was a very peaceful city, she was not used to the place. In addition, at this time of year, it was packed with tourists. Gabriela was a beautiful girl and very credulous ... he felt a shiver at the thought of something bad happening to her.

"She'll need it very early tomorrow to place an order" - she replied, shifting the appliance to the other arm.

"Um..." - he muttered and suddenly decided. - "I will go with you."

"Wh, what?"

"I'm coming with you."

"But you don't like going out. Neither people."

He laughed.

"In that way it seems that I am an antisocial."

She arched her brow.

"Yes, sir *Visitors are only welcome when invited?*"

He laughed as he remembered the words he said the first time he saw her.

"It seems that you are being a bad influence for me. I feel almost sociable."

"Really?" - She asked in disbelief. - "Please don't bite

the child. Your social skills are very similar to those of a Pinscher.”

Samuca laughed.

“Are you being ironic?”

She smiled sweetly.

“I think I’m not the only bad influence here.”

He approached her, their bodies separated only by the mixer she was hugging. Samuca leaned over and spoke softly as he stroked her cheek with his forefinger.

“Don’t ever change, Gabriela.”

She nodded, unsure and not sure how to respond. That proximity left her shaking and panting. Samuca aroused unknown feelings, which she did not know how to deal with. Why was it that every time he came so close, her heart raced?

Then he kissed the top of her head and took a step back.

“Let’s go?” - He asked, and she nodded.

The two left and started walking to Judith’s house.

With a mug of hot chocolate in his hands, Samuca looked around the simple house, wondering how he had never noticed that place so close to his cottage. He shouldn’t be surprised. Since he moved to that isolated place, he didn’t really understand what was going on in the world. He was lost in a fog of anger, hurt and pain, which didn’t leave much room for him to notice other things.

He took a long sip of the drink, which tasted of childhood, home and comfort - memories of when he was a child and his mother prepared the drink for him and his brother -, listening to the animated voices of Gabriela and Judith in the kitchen.

His thoughts turned to the moment when he and Gabriela had arrived. Judith opened the door with a big smile and didn't seem surprised to find him there, quite the opposite. The woman, who must have been about forty years old, pulled him into a tight hug and made him sit in the living room, pushing the mug in his hand as she took Gabriela into the kitchen to show her something she had prepared. Before leaving the room, she let him know her husband would be arriving soon and recommended that he made himself comfortable.

Taking another sip of the drink, he felt someone's presence. Looking in the corridor's direction, which led to the other rooms of the small house, he saw a little boy, who should not have been more than six years old, with curly hair and black skin, very different from Judith, who had straight blond hair - she seemed to have Germanic descent, very present in the region.

The little boy continued to stare at him, and he swallowed, thinking about what he should do. Then he smiled and offered him the chocolate, who shook his head, but took a few steps, approaching.

"Hi" - the boy said, with a smile without the two front teeth. - "Who are you?"

Without knowing how to explain, he decided to be as simple as possible.

"I'm Samuca."

The little boy's smile widened, and he came even closer, climbed on his lap and sat down.

"My name is Roberto, I am six years old and Aunt Gabriela said that you know how to tell stories to kids like me."

Samuca opened and closed his mouth, surprised by the boy's resourcefulness and confidence.

"I... um... write books."

"Are you a *real* writer? Really?"

Samuca nodded, feeling a lump form in his throat.

"I swear it."

"Can you tell me a story?" - He asked and snuggled closer to the man, who nodded. Thinking for a few moments, he decided to tell a little about the adventures of his new character, remembering that Gabriela had said that someone else should evaluate his story. Nothing should be better than a little boy thirsty for a little adventure, right?

After a while, which Samuca did not know how to measure - it could have been a few minutes or even hours -, in which the two were lost in the fantastic universe he had created, the sound of a door being opened sounded and the little boy stood up from his lap like a lightning, running to welcome the father who was entering.

"Daddy, there's a *real* writer in our house! And he has a character called Robert! He said it is my name in English. And he participates in many adventures when he crosses the

magic portal! It's awesome!!" - The man laughed and took the boy on his lap, hugging him. He looked in the direction of Samuca, who stood up to greet him.

They shook hands, and Milton settled on the other couch with the little boy on his lap. Roberto couldn't stop talking, excited about the conversation he was having with Samuca before his father arrived. The guy observed father and son, noting that they looked alike. They had the same eyes, nose and mouth shapes. The father's hair was wavy and the brown skin was much lighter than the boy's. It was clear that Roberto was his son, but not Judith's. Samuca watched the man closely, seeing the small wrinkles that formed around his eyes, the lines of concern on his forehead and the tired look.

Judith called the boy from the kitchen, and he ran off, leaving the two alone.

"You look tired... if you prefer to take a shower and relax, don't worry about me. I'm just waiting for Gabriela to come home."

The man's eyes softened when he heard about the girl.

"This girl is an angel." - Samuca nodded. - "Don't worry - I'm fine... just a little tired. I left early to look for a job, but the market is very difficult."

"What did you work on?"

"For years, I worked as an administrator of a small hotel in Canela. But with the economic crisis, they closed the hotel, and I ended up losing my job." - He shrugged.

"I'm so sorry..." - Samuca muttered, and the man nodded.

The two continued to talk for a long time, and Samuca

was surprised by the affinity that developed quickly between the two. Gabriela was right. His neighbors were good people.

"What bothers me the most is being overloading my wife, you know? Since I lost my job, she has taken responsibility for our livelihood. She is a great cook. She has been taking orders for sweets and snacks for parties. She spends the whole day standing in that kitchen and takes care of Roberto while I go out to look for a job."

"She is an admirable woman" - Samuca said, and the man nodded.

"More than you can imagine..." - he leaned back on the sofa, sighed and spoke again. - "Judith is the most amazing and kind woman I have ever met. Someone so capable of loving and forgiving without measure, that it makes me wish every day to be a better man and to be able to offer the world to her..."

Then, he faced Samuca.

"Have you been together for a long time?"

The man nodded.

"We were boyfriends in our teens. We were in love with each other. But a young boy, you know how it goes. Wants to party... fun. I broke up, left town and went to enjoy life. Until the girl I was dating got pregnant. She had a serious birth complication and died. I was alone with that little baby and ended up returning to the city. The first person I met was Judith." - He smiled. - "Reviewing that smile made me realize that I had never stopped loving her. But I thought our chance was in the past, since I had a child now." - With teary eyes, Milton went on. - "But she showed me that true

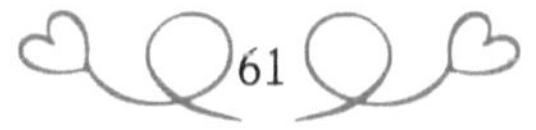

love resists anything. That when we love and are loved, we can face the world and become better people. She took my son as hers and the love she has for him is as deep as what she shows for me. They are so close that they look like a real mother and child."

Judith entered the room hand in hand with little Roberto, followed closely by Gabriela. She sat next to her husband, who put his arm around her.

"But we are real mother and son, my love. Isn't that right, Roberto?"

"Sure" - said the little boy, with a toothless smile.

"Love is the strongest link between two people, regardless of genetic link."

He kissed the woman's forehead and muttered to her:

"I don't deserve you..."

"Of course you deserve it, stop being silly," - she said with a laugh in her voice and nudged her husband. - "You need to stop blaming yourself for taking a detour along the way. If you hadn't done that, I wouldn't have my beloved loved little boy here." - She tickled the boy's belly, who laughed happily.

Then she looked at Samuca, who seemed touched by their words. He felt very guilty about everything that had happened. Would he ever be able to forgive himself and those who had hurt him so much?

"In life, we all make mistakes. It is how we deal with these mistakes that makes us who we are."

Samuca felt Gabriela's hand, which was sitting on the arm of the chair beside her, squeeze his and intertwined her fingers with his.

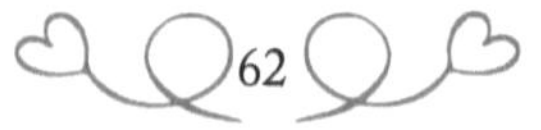

Six

Ninth day

Pacing around the room, Gabriela was feeling uncomfortable. It was a few days before Christmas and there was nothing in the cottage to show it. She loved seeing the city decorated for the holidays with shining lights, colorful Christmas trees, Santa Claus, reindeers and everything else that made that party so beautiful.

Samuca would not be recovered without letting the magic of Christmas in, she thought to herself. It made her smile. She was satisfied with the progress of the guy, who had reduced the amount of notes and coins he deposited in the swearing jar, proof that he was less irritable and more relaxed. In the past few days, they had come even closer. They had deep conversations about life and feelings. To her satisfaction, she had won the writer's trust and felt that her own feelings towards him grew day by day, which left her confused.

Marcela, her friend in a new position, had said that

angels should always keep a distance from humans or they took the risk of developing unacceptable affections, after all it was impossible for an angel and a human to have long-term relationships of any kind.

Pushing those thoughts away, Gabriela went to the office, where Samuca had been staring at the computer for the last half hour, and called him.

"Put on your shoes. Let's go" - She said and left the room.

"Hey, where are we going?" - He asked, going after her down the hall.

When she turned, the man felt short of breath.

"To the city."

Her smile seemed to have lit up the hall. Feeling impacted by her beauty, he nodded silently. Gabriela had only been in his life for twelve days and he could no longer deny her anything. The girl enthralled him, enveloped him, was helping him to get up to move on, and for the first time since he moved into the cottage, he felt that his life was about to change inevitably. For better.

At the end of the day, Samuca and Gabriela were excited and laughed like two children. They had bought a big Christmas tree, blinkers, garlands and Christmas ornaments. After shopping, they stopped at a cafe in the gastronomic center and were drinking hot chocolate when they met Alex, his friend who owns the bookshop in Curitiba, and Jade, his wife, who owned a famous cake shop.

"What a surprise to find them here!" - Samuca exclaimed when he saw the couple.

They greeted each other and the boy introduced Gabriela to the two, who sat at the same table. During the conversation, Jade explained that she had gone there in search of a business opportunity.

"I am working to expand my cake shop through franchises. I came to talk to some traders in the region, but I was unsuccessful."

"Franchises? How interesting" - Samuca said, and Jade nodded.

"What's that?" - Gabriela asked. Jade and Alex explained, not only what franchise was, but what they were looking for.

"Anyway" - Alex said - "Jade wants to find someone dedicated and who has the same love for cooking as she does."

"I know it doesn't seem very... um... professional... but I want to find people who fit my company's philosophy and who I feel are the right ones for the business."

Samuca was silent for a while and then spoke, surprising everyone.

"I will propose something, but feel free to refuse."

Jade and Alex looked at each other, and Gabriela turned to him.

"I know the right person to run your business here in Gramado..." - he said. - "Judith is great..."

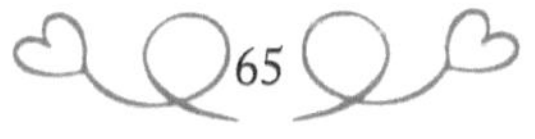

He was interrupted by Gabriela, whose eyes shone. She started to clap.

"Judith! My God, she is wonderful."

Samuca continued to talk about Judith, and Jade perked up.

"I would love to meet her!"

"Um, but do you think she will be able to invest in a business like this, Samuca? From what you said, she is a woman of simple life..." - Alex asked.

Samuca smiled, feeling that, for the first time in a long time, he was doing something right.

"She, not. But nothing a partner with money to invest cannot do" - he said and smiled.

Gabriela turned to him, gaping.

"You? Can you invest in it? Do you have all that money?" - She asked, confused. Gabriela had no idea how much it would take to start a company, but from the way Alex spoke, she imagined it was too much. During her time on Earth, she learned a little about the importance of money in people's lives.

"Well, I'm going to need to do something with the money in that pot, won't I?" - He laughed. - "Besides, the royalties I received from my last book are still the bank. It seems interesting to me to invest in a business that I know can be profitable and that has already worked in another region."

The four talked a little more about the business, until Samuca invited them to meet Judith in person.

They were hanging the ornaments on the Christmas tree when Gabriela said:

"Judith and her husband were so happy. It was really beautiful what you did for them."

Samuca waved his hand, discarding.

"Jade's company is very solid and known throughout the country. It will be a good investment" - he replied, minimizing what he had done while hanging a ball on a high branch. - "Judith is an excellent cook and Milton has a lot of experience in running businesses."

"A good investment and a chance to be supportive and support people who need help. I was proud of you."

Samuca stopped what he was doing and looked at her. He felt a chill all over his body and a feeling of peace like never before. He remembered the conversation with Milton and thought that Gabriela did for him exactly what the man described about Judith: she made him want to be someone better. Someone worthy of her pride and trust. Each day, she rescued him from the shadows and brought him into the light.

Gabriela looked at him and it was as if something magical enveloped them. They stared at each other for a few moments, unable to look away, in total silence. Then he raised his hand and caressed her face. She snuggled into his hand, accepting the affectionate stroking. The barriers that he had raised during all those months of pain and agony

were gradually broken down by that sweet, caring and special girl.

Gabriela knew she needed to walk away. She was sure that whatever was going on between them did not fit that distance that she should maintain. But she couldn't. She didn't have enough strength to refuse to feel his touch. She couldn't walk away, and if she was honest with herself, she didn't want to. She wanted to know that form of love that she never experienced and that she did not believe she would have a chance to find one day.

So, she decided to surrender herself to the moment, at the touch of Samuca and enjoy what life was offering. She knew that her time with him was limited. In a few days, she would have to say goodbye and return to her world. But she would take those moments of happiness with her. Stolen moments from the time when only the two mattered.

Everything around them stopped when their lips met in a kiss. They knew it was a unique moment and that they would remember it forever. As their mouths came together, Samuca could only think that he felt as if he had came home. That, finally, after the storm, he had found his way back. He wrapped his arms around her waist, who stood on her tiptoes and he wrapped around her neck, deepening the kiss.

When their lips parted, the two held each other, with their heads against each other's, eyes closed and panting, lost in that whirlwind of emotions. But while Samuca felt he was in the right place and with the right girl for him, Gabriela could only ask for time to pass slowly. Really slowly...

Seven

Eleventh day

Samuca and Gabriela no longer came apart. They plunged into a routine in which the world seemed to revolve only around them and that was enough for them. The days together were sweet, romantic, full of laughter and joy. They worked on the manuscript of the new book, which was now in its final stretch, cooked together and talked a lot.

He taught her to use her cell phone, which amazed her. She learned to send a text message and couldn't stop sending cute faces to him on the device. They watched movies at night, especially Christmas movies, which she found to be her favorites. Their lives were perfect - except for the fact that she knew she would be gone in four days.

Without wanting to think about it, after all she didn't want to suffer in anticipation, she got out of the bath, put on a colorful shirt, pink pants and was drying her long hair when she heard a knock on the door.

"You can come in" - she said and met Samuca's eyes in the mirror of her room. She smiled at him and when she watched him closely, she saw that he was wearing a beautiful dark suit. "Wow..." she muttered, and he laughed.

"I've brought you this."

Only then did she realize that he was holding a coat-covered hanger.

"What is it?" - She stood up and approached him, who kissed her on the lips.

"A dress."

"Oh," she muttered, surprised by the gift. - "Are we going out?"

He nodded.

"If you don't mind..."

Her smile widened.

"I'm going to change clothes."

He blinked, kissed her lips again and spoke before leaving:

"See you down there."

Gabriela was too enthralled with the long baby pink dress, filled with shiny little beads to realize where they were going. Only when he climbed the steps and linked his arm with hers, she realized that they were in a sacred temple. It was a church – the God's house on Earth. They started walking down the corridor, but she slowed down, impressed

by everything she saw there. It was beautiful, with many angels painted on the ceiling and it was all decorated with flowers.

She looked towards the altar and was surprised to see Nico looking at them, wearing a suit as elegant as his brother's.

"But what ..." she muttered.

"Let's marry my brother" - Samuca spoke proudly.

When they reached the altar, her eyes filled with tears, so did Nico's, who could hardly believe that Samuca was there. They both knew this was a big step for the guy who had suffered so much in the past few months. But that was the proof that true love had the power to transform. It was incredible to see that this man, who had been hurt so deeply, had managed to overcome his own pain and participate in the most special moment of his brother's life without suffering. As it should be. Gabriela couldn't help feeling proud of her work until now. For the first time, she was successfully fulfilling a mission, even though the consequence was an imminent separation.

When the bride entered the church in a beautiful dress and her face was lit with happiness, Gabriela could not contain her tears of emotion. She was witnessing one of humanity's most romantic moments, when a woman was forever united with her beloved. She sighed, and Samuca looked at her, watching the tears slide down her pretty face. He raised his hand, wiped her face with his fingertips and gave her a soft kiss.

Snuggled up to him while watching Nico and Josie to

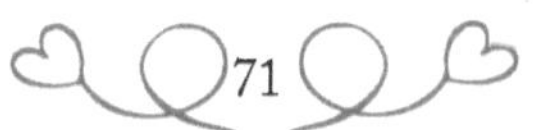

promise eternal love, Gabriela allowed herself to dream a little bit as what would be if she could be with Samuca forever. She had no doubt that it would be perfect.

Clink clink clink.

The unmistakable sound of a fork hitting a glass of champagne caught the attention of everyone, who turned to the table of the newlyweds, where the best men were also accommodated, and they found Samuca standing, microphone in hand.

"Good evening, ladies and gentlemen" - he began his speech. - "As best man and brother of the groom, I could start by saying that I saw the relationship between Nico and Josie being born, grow and flourish. That they are the most perfect couple for each other that I know and that I am sure that they will have that kind of family that gets to irritate people, so happy that they will be." - Everyone laughed at his joke. - "But we all know that. What I mean here is that Nico is my brother, but he was also my father and my best friend. He helped my mother raise me and when she departed, he kept his word to never leave me. And he never really left me. Not when I became intractable during adolescence, nor when I pushed him away with all my strength after a great disappointment. He was by my side the whole time and never gave up on me. He's one of the best guys I know and deserves all the love that Josie devotes to him."

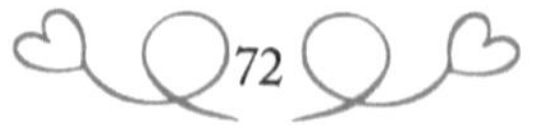

Gabriela wiped away a tear that escaped, thrilled to see him opening himself like that in the name of love for his brother.

"I know I don't say that often, Nico. Maybe I didn't even say. But I love you."

Nico stood up and hugged him tightly, touched.

"I love you too, man. You can't imagine how much it - your presence and your words - meant to me."

Josie joined them and hugged him too.

"It was worth not losing my faith" - she muttered to Samuca, who kissed his sister-in-law's forehead tenderly.

When they got home, very late that night, Samuca smiled when he saw Gabriela's face light up with the flasher on. He found it incredible that she kept that sparkle in her eyes whenever she saw the big Christmas tree.

"It was a wonderful night" - she said, taking off her shoes.

"It was," he said. - "But it doesn't have to end now."

"No?" - she arched her brow.

He shook his head, held out his hand to her and smiled.

"Do you want to dance with me?" - He asked, and she nodded excitedly, standing and allowing herself to be wrapped around his arms.

Whispering a Christmas song in her ear, he hugged her tenderly and the two danced - and kissed - in front of the tree until dawn.

Eight

Twelveth day

While Gabriela was reading the scenes he had written that morning, Samuca went downtown to buy her chocolate donuts. He thought it was amazing that she came from a place where there weren't such common things for him, like cell phones and donuts. Who in the world could not have eaten something so delicious, for God's sake?

He parked the car in a parking space in front of the bakery and was about to enter the store when he bumped into a man.

"I'm sorry" - he said. When he looked at the man's face, he met the green eyes of Marco, the former friend. His first reaction was to turn around and leave, but he remembered everything he had been talking to Gabriela since she arrived at his house. - "Marco," - he greeted, nodding his head.

"Samuca, my fr..." - the other man started, but he interrupted him.

"Please, don't call me that."

Marco nodded with sad eyes.

"During the past few months, you asked me for a chance to speak... to justify yourself - if what you both did has any justification. I wasn't ready to hear you, but ... now I am. Go ahead." - He tilted his head slightly to the side. - "Well, that is, if it's still your interest to say something."

The man opened his eyes wide, surprised.

"Sure. Well, that was unexpected." - He took a deep breath. - "Can we sit down?" - He indicated one of the tables outside the bakery.

After settling in, Marco ran a hand through his brown hair.

"I know that what happened hurt you a lot. The moment I allowed it to happen, I knew I screwed up with everything. From everything wrong I've ever done in my life, this is what I regret the most, man."

Samuca watched him with an expressionless face. He thought that when he heard Marco speak, he would be angry, that he would feel all that anger boiling up inside him again. Now, all he felt was indifference. It was as if it all of that had happened in another life.

"Are you together?" - He asked out of curiosity.

"What? No of course not." - Marco shook his head. - "I haven't seen her since that... well, that happened. I heard she left town, but I never spoke to her again."

"Was it your idea? Hers?"

"I don't know. Of the two, I think. You know how Leticia was. She liked to woo everyone, always very friendly.

Honestly, I don't know why it happened. But I need to ask for your forgiveness. I can't believe I threw our friendship out the window."

Samuca was silent for a few moments as he nodded, considering the man's words.

"Sorry..." - he muttered. - "Listen, Marco, I don't know why you want my forgiveness. It's just words that will not change what happened. The betrayal of you both changed everything. It changed me. It completely transformed the person I was, and that Samuel from the past will never return. But I learned to deal with the events and your attitude." - He was silent for a few more moments, then continued. - "I think that when I managed to overcome the bad feelings that accompanied me, I managed to *forgive* you. But I will never forget. I cannot and do not want to be your 'friend' or client again. The trust that existed between us has broken and there is no way to collect the pieces."

"I understand and appreciate the opportunity to be able to speak to you and apologize appropriately."

Samuca nodded, got up and went into the bakery. Finally, that stage of his life was completely over.

When Samuca came home with the donuts, he told Gabriela what had happened. She encouraged him to say what he was feeling, and he said he was relieved to no longer feel that deep hatred that consumed him. That he was much

calmer now and that he believed that conversation was all that was needed to leave the past behind for good.

And when he went to the kitchen to make coffee for sweets, Gabriela closed herself in the bathroom and cried. Those were tears of joy, knowing that his broken heart was healed, but also of sadness, for she knew that her time there was ending much faster than she would have liked.

Nine

Fourteenth day – a few hours before midnight.

As Nico and Josie were on their honeymoon and would only return to spend New Year's Eve at home, Samuca and Gabriela prepared a Christmas meal just for the two of them. Earlier, they had received Judith, Milton and Roberto, who brought Christmas presents to be placed in the big tree in the room and took the opportunity to tell how things were going with Jade. Samuca would be a silent partner. He would make the financial investment, but he would leave the business to the two.

It was clear what that opportunity had done to the couple's self-esteem. They were very happy to have the chance to work together on something they believed in. It was like a dream coming true, and they were very grateful for everything Samuca had done for them.

After the romantic Christmas dinner, by candlelight, Samuca took the Kindle and handed it to Gabriela.

"I know it's Christmas Eve and everything, but I need you to read it."

She laughed, and they settled on the couch. Gabriela snuggled up to his chest and read the last pages of his manuscript. He was sure that this was his best book and although she had not read any other book before, he believed that the story was incredible, inspiring and exciting.

"It's wonderful, Samuca. You've made it!"

They hugged and kissed. This time, it was a kiss more intense and deeper than those they used to exchange. But Gabriela knew she needed to talk to him. She had little time now, and he needed to understand what was going to happen. Which would not be easy.

"I need to talk to you about one thing," - she said -, "but I'm not sure where to start."

He brushed a lock of her hair behind her ear.

"You can say whatever you want, I'm very interested in hear it," he said playfully. She straightened up on the couch, sitting up and building up the courage to have the most difficult conversation in life.

"You won't believe it ..." she muttered, and he frowned.

"You won't tell me you're compromised," - he said seriously, and she shook her head.

"No, no. Of course not."

"You can say whatever it is. I'll take your word for it."

She nodded, inhaled and asked.

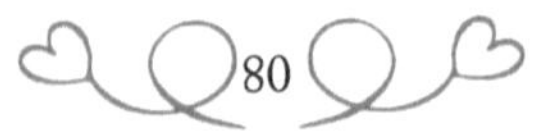

"Do you remember when I arrived here? That JP told you that I would only stay until Christmas?"

"Yes, but obviously that has changed, hasn't it?" - He asked, arching an eyebrow, not understanding what she was getting at. They were happy together, weren't they? There was no reason to leave.

But Gabriela shook her head.

"Unfortunately, not."

"Will you leave me?" - Samuca asked, impatient. Then he got up. - "I can't believe you earned my trust, made me open up to you and fall in love to leave."

Gabriela's eyes filled with tears.

"It's not like this..."

"So how is it?"

She stood up, tears streaming down her face, took his hand and made him sit down again.

"I couldn't tell you. I don't even know what the consequences of my words will be, but I can't leave without you understanding."

"Gabriela, you're scaring me."

"Fine. But don't say I didn't warn you." - He looked at her impatiently. - "I am an angel."

"What? What are you talking about?"

Then Gabriela told. Word by word. She told the whole truth about where she came from and who she was. As expected, Samuca did not believe.

"Are you thinking I look like an idiot?" - he screamed. - "If you didn't want to be with me, just talk. There was no

need to invent this ridiculous story of angel, heaven, mission and guardians."

She looked at the clock on the living room shelf and saw the hand approaching midnight.

"You must believe me. I'm not going because I want to, I'm going because I need to. I am not from this world and I do not believe they will allow me to stay."

"I should have followed my intuition when you got here. I noticed you were crazy, with that pot and all, but I let myself go."

Her tears were falling steadily, but she didn't have much time left.

"I'm not crazy. I'm an angel who fell in love with you. And if I had a choice, I would trade my eternity to live here, with you, for as long as I was allowed, but that choice was not given to me."

She approached him, who was also crying when he heard her words.

"I love you, Samuca. I really love. Forgive me..."

The needle struck midnight and lightning flashed outside, drawing Samuca's attention to the window. When he looked back at Gabriela, he saw that he was alone. She had magically disappeared.

"Like an angel who returned to heaven..." - he muttered. - "No, noooo" - he shouted in despair, realizing that as strange as all that was, it was true. And he hadn't believed her.

He ran to the window, looking for something outside. One sign, one last sight of her, but he found nothing.

Feeling despair overwhelming him when he realized he

had lost his great love, he did what he hadn't done in a long time. So much that he didn't even remember how. Crying, he knelt and prayed.

"Please, God, bring her back to me. Please, please."

And despite having asked with much fervor, he continued alone.

Ten

Fifteenth day – just after midnight.

"I recommended it so much that you didn't tell anyone about us," Angela complained when she saw her in front of him.

Gabriela blinked slowly, focusing on the guardian.

"Oh, dear, I'm back," - she muttered, feeling tears slide down her cheek.

"Of course you're back. Here's your place. What did you expect?"

"To stay with him" - she replied without hesitation.

Angela looked serious and watched her for a while without saying a word, until she asked.

"Was what you said down there true?"

"What?" - Gabriela asked, but she didn't even need to. She didn't lie to anyone. Ever.

"That you would trade your eternity to live with him for the time you were given?" - She asked, very seriously.

"I would give anything to stay with him and live that love."

"Even your eternity?" - Angela asked. That was something really serious.

"Even my eternity" - Gabriela agreed.

The guardian led her to another room, where all the other guardians were. Upon entering, she opened her eyes wide, worried about what would happen. What kind of punishment would she receive for not fulfilling what was determined?

Angela sat down, and Gabriela stood, facing all the guardians. She bowed his head in a sign of respect. Miguel asked her to look at them and started talking:

"As one of our angels, Gabriela, you know that there are rules that we must respect for our own safety."

"Yes, sir" - she muttered.

"That's why we avoid sending you to Earth. We never know what can happen." - He shrugged. - "Sometimes, things get out of control, and you don't respect these rules created for your own safety."

"I'm sorry to disappoint you" - she muttered.

But Miguel kept talking.

"And at other times, you find the lost soul mates."

Gabriela looked up again and rubbed the back of her hand over her face to keep the tears away.

"It's what happened, isn't it?" - He asked, and she nodded

again. - "Then I will ask, in front of all the guardians, and according to your answer, your fate will be sealed."

She nodded.

"Gabriela, do you want to give up your eternity to live on Earth?"

"Yes, yes, yes!" - she exclaimed, not believing that it was really happening.

Miguel raised his hand and, suddenly, everything went out.

Eleven

The first day of the rest of their lives

Samuca blinked slowly when the first rays of sunlight crossed the curtain and woke him. His head and body hurt. Remembering the events of the night before, he closed his eyes again. He still couldn't believe that his whole world was gone right before his nose.

He turned in bed, determined to go back to sleep, but the strong smell of fresh coffee intrigued him.

"But what…" - he muttered to himself as he got up from the bed and went to the kitchen barefoot, wearing only his pajama pants.

In the hall, he heard a tuned voice sing *Santa Claus is coming to town*. He rubbed his eyes and picked up his pace. It wasn't possible. His subconscious was playing tricks on him.

But when he entered the kitchen, he stopped when he walked through the door and saw the little blonde with long hair falling in waves, wearing a dress as colorful as a rainbow and who was facing the sink, singing and rummaging in the rhythm from music.

She turned suddenly, making him lose his breath.

"Good morning. Want a coffee?" - Gabriela asked with a small smile, as if she hadn't disappeared right before his eyes the day before.

He went to her and pulled her close to him, hugging her tightly.

"Am I dreaming?" - he asked. - "Are you real?"

"So much so that I'm almost suffocating," - she replied and laughed.

He picked her up and turned her around in the kitchen while they laughed happily together.

"But how... what..." - he tried to ask, but she put her hand on his lips.

"We made a deal. And now I'm here."

He became serious, realizing the seriousness of what she had done.

"You traded your eternity..." - he started, but was interrupted again, this time with two hands over his lips.

"Shhhh." - She smiled. - "I traded a lonely eternity for a life of love with you. But if you keep complaining, I'll trade you for a donut."

Samuca hugged her again and laughed.

"If I promise to give you an unlimited supply of donuts, will you stay with me?"

"If you promise to stay with me, I'll give you the world.

Our world" - she said, and Samuca felt his heart fill with love.

"I love you, Gabriela."

"I love you too, Samuca."

Their lips met, and they were lost in a passionate kiss. Until Gabriela interrupted him:

"Did you send the manuscript to JP?"

He grimaced.

"Do you want to talk about work now that I'm kissing my girl?"

She pushed him out of the kitchen and walked with him towards the office.

"Your girl won't go anywhere without you. But your manuscript needs to be handed over on time."

"Okay, okay."

After the email was sent, Samuca and Gabriela went on to live their happily ever after.

Together.

As it should be.

The End.

Warning

No angel was sacrificed while this book was being written. Well, except for Gabriela's wings.

Acknowledgments

In order for me to give this *One Magical Christmas* to my readers, it was necessary the support, encouragement and help of some real-life angels.

To start, I can't help but thank Alessandra Ruiz, my agent. You gave me exactly what I needed without even knowing it: a challenge. And God knows how I adore them. Thank you for the opportunity and for believing that I could achieve the goal in such a short time.

Lu, my friend, sister, book cover designer, partner, daily company and with whom I exchange the best memes on the internet: thank you for being all that and more. You never doubt my ability and embark on these adventures with me with such confidence that I truly believe I am capable of everything. Thanks for the amazing cover, as usual, and for having Job's patience when I don't like anything. You're the best!

Thank you, Felipe, my love, for the encouragement. You hear me talking about this whole universe that is not part of your routine, but that you embraced as yours when I decided to follow the books' path. I love you.

To the best readers in the world - mine, of course! - thank you so much for all your support and love. I hope your Christmas will be a little more special with this reading. Keep being awesome!

To the #BlogAmigos, my very special thanks. You are the best partners in the world and I am very proud of you.